"Graceful images, scenes, and dialogue blossom, meaning *Malagash* rings with authentic emotion . . . Comeau gives readers a spare novel that feels real when it counts."
— *Toronto Star*

"[A] sly and affecting novella . . . Comeau grasps a crucial truth that the most important characters in fiction about death are the survivors, and this book ends not with visions of the deluge but the promise of the rainbow sign."
— *Wall Street Journal*, Best New Fiction

"Giving us a glimpse into small town Nova Scotia, Comeau's story of a teenage girl who refuses to accept her father's impending death is beautifully crafted and darkly funny."
— CBC Books

"A spare, ice pick–sharp look at coping with death . . . A fine fable for all smart readers."
— *Library Journal*

"*Malagash* is a unique take on death in the digital age. Comeau presents a forthright yet eloquent story about life, death, and what we leave behind. Highly recommended."
— *Atlantic Books Today*

"A glimpse of Sunday's family was all it took for me to be invested in this preteen girl and her introspective journey through the pain of a parent's illness."
— *Canadian Living*

"Witty and poignant . . . It perfectly captures the all-too-relatable feeling of dealing with loss. . . Comeau's fragmented sentences and short chapters provide a darkly humorous yet thoughtful read — one that will leave you feeling melancholy long after you're done."
— *THIS Magazine*

"*Malagash* is an unexpected little book, a slim novella by Joey Comeau. Full of wit and punch and wisdom . . . Comeau's writing is pithy, and filled with flashes of delight and sadness. The characters, even when overheard from a distance, inspire affectionate and knowing smiles from the reader. *Malagash* lets air and light — and laughter — into the room of grief."
— *Scene Magazine*

"Original, tender, and tightly written, *Malagash* is funny and smart, but also deeply moving."
— Open Book

"*Malagash* offers a contemporary narrative about grief and the complex emotional struggle it engenders . . . Comeau creates his own kind of virus with his prose, something I haven't been able to shake off since reading."
— *Strange Horizons*

"It's an escape for these characters that is explored to touching effect by Comeau's tranquil, lyrical prose . . . Comeau's novel lingers with its small pithy truths, its big pithy truths, and all the stuff in between."
— *The Coast*

Malagash !!

*Also by Joey Comeau*

FICTION

A SOFTER WORLD BOOKS (with Emily Horne)

C:\MALAGASH>book.exe

# MALAGASH

JOEY COMEAU

ECW

Published by ECW Press
665 Gerrard Street East
Toronto, Ontario, Canada M4M 1Y2
416-694-3348 / info@ecwpress.com

Get the
eBook free!*
*proof of purchase
required

Purchase the print edition
and receive the eBook free!
For details, go to ecwpress.com/eBook.

LIBRARY AND ARCHIVES CANADA
CATALOGUING IN PUBLICATION

Comeau, Joey, 1980–, author
Malagash / Joey Comeau.

Issued in print and electronic formats.
ISBN 978-1-77041-407-5 (softcover)
ALSO ISSUED AS: 978-1-77305-109-3 (PDF)
978-1-77305-110-9 (ePUB)
I. TITLE.
PS8605.O537M35 2017     C813'.6
C2017-902410-8     C2017-902989-4

Editors for the press: Crissy Calhoun
and Laura Pastore
Cover design: Michel Vrana
Cover photos: ocean storm © DKart/iStock-
Photo; sunset over the sea © mycola/iStockPhoto

The publication of *Malagash* has been generously supported by the Canada Council for the Arts,
which last year invested $153 million to bring the arts to Canadians throughout the country, and by the
Government of Canada through the Canada Book Fund. *Nous remercions le Conseil des arts du Canada
de son soutien. L'an dernier, le Conseil a investi 153 millions de dollars pour mettre de l'art dans la vie des
Canadiennes et des Canadiens de tout le pays. Ce livre est financé en partie par le gouvernement du Canada.*
We also acknowledge the support of the Ontario Arts Council (OAC), an agency of the Government
of Ontario, which last year funded 1,737 individual artists and 1,095 organizations in 223 communities
across Ontario for a total of $52.1 million, and the contribution of the Government of Ontario through
the Ontario Book Publishing Tax Credit and the Ontario Media Development Corporation.
The author would also like to thank the Writers Trust of Canada and the Woodcock Fund.

Ontario
Ontario Media Development
Corporation

ONTARIO ARTS COUNCIL
CONSEIL DES ARTS DE L'ONTARIO
an Ontario government agency
un organisme du gouvernement de l'Ontario

Canada Council
for the Arts

Conseil des Arts
du Canada

Canadä

PRINTED AND BOUND IN CANADA          PRINTING: MARQUIS    5    4    3    2

RECYCLED
Paper made from
recycled material
FSC
www.fsc.org    FSC® C103567

*for my mother, Karen Byers*

-- ONE --

>_

"A weight will lift." My father has a big cup of crushed ice that he keeps tilting side to side. It hasn't melted enough yet. "A weight will lift," he says.

He's tired of having to say "I know" in that reassuring voice, again and again. "I know, Sunday. I know." So he's found this new way of saying it. "A weight will lift. A leaf will fall. Fresh white snow will blanket this whole sleepy town."

"That's very poetic," I tell him.

He tilts his crushed ice again.

"Sunday, you are my daughter," he says, holding out his hand for mine. I take it. "You are my daughter," he says, "and it breaks my heart that the day has finally come for you to learn this hard and simple truth."

His face is very serious, which is one of the ways my father smiles. He pauses, as though he's searching for just the right words. He isn't searching, of course. Nothing comes easier to my father than teasing me.

"The truth is that we, each and every one of us, get old and frail, Sunday. We, each and every one of us, lie down in the winter of our lives," he tilts his ice, "to make way for the baby skunks and the excitable little porcupines which are born in the spring." He says this in his hospital bed, wearing a flimsy bathrobe. His face is deadly earnest. He thinks he is so funny. "Poking their heads up through the frost, because it is their time now, my darling daughter. It is their time now to glitter in the sun." Squeezing my hand like on TV.

"That's very poetic," I tell him again.

"You said that already," my father says.

"*Very* poetic," I say.

It's my own fault for saying the same thing every day. I don't want you to die. I don't want you to die.

"Snow will blanket the town," he says, solemnly.

"Snow in the middle of July?" I say. "Oh wow, like in a metaphor?"

"Sometimes the winter comes earlier than we want," my father says. "Sometimes the sky—"

"Okay, enough with the—" I stop myself. This is infuriating. It is meant to be infuriating. My father smiles at the crack in my voice, takes a sip from his melting crushed ice. And once again, I can see that I am arguing against death itself. A stubborn child. A little girl. I don't *want* a weight to lift. I don't *want* a leaf to fall.

It doesn't matter how stupid my father's arguments are, how clichéd his metaphors. He's on the winning side. The cancer is everywhere. In two weeks, maybe a month, we'll have reached the end of this twisting garden path. And he will prove me wrong. A weight will lift. A leaf will fall. Fresh white snow will blanket this whole stupid town.

>_

I thought Malagash would be a small town, but it is not even that. One long road, a twisting red paved loop around the north shore of Nova Scotia. There's a tractor sitting in a field. A dirt bike leaning up against a shed. We pass a pen of llamas, who look bored as hell. The Atlantic Ocean itself comes right up to drive along beside us. Then it slips away.

In the front seat I have my phone out again. The glass and metal object that was once my phone. I've got nobody left to call. Which is a relief, because I've got no energy left to pretend. There are only so many condolences a body can sit through. Only so many updates on what you've missed before you don't miss it.

I use my phone to record my mother. The thunk of potholes. Shaky video glimpses of the cottages slipping past. The waif humming to himself. The trees rushing. It records everything it can while we drive through my father's hometown for the first time. Prim little houses spaced for privacy, each sitting on its own beautiful view of the sea. There's an old general store with a dying neon PIZZA sign.

My mother's voice plays over the mud. The mud stretches out to the green-grey ocean.

"A *community* is the polite term," she says. "An elephants' graveyard for people." Laughter in her voice, like when she teases us. This place is family to her. Neither Simon nor I have ever been here, but my mom and dad had a whole life. They lived here together, before Simon or I were born. With the phone up to the window, I record what I can. There is a church, a vineyard, an abandoned salt mine somewhere beneath us, a bible camp, a wharf where lobster fishermen once set out to sea. Maybe they still do? Another wharf. Another. Wharves always look abandoned. There's a real graveyard on both sides of the church. "Those plots are as far as some of these people ever go," my mother says as we pass.

Some facts my mother remembers:

"The road is red like this from clay. They used what they had. Look how red the dirt is, too."

"When the tide is out, you can walk forever and only ever get up to your waist."

"Those cottages there belonged to your father's aunt Edie and uncle Harry. Separate cottages right next door to one another. Isn't that perfect? It saved their marriage."

There was no need to convince us to move here. We didn't plead or fight. Our father wanted to go home to Nova Scotia, to die near his mother and his childhood memories. We wanted to be with our father. The math was simple enough. Take us anywhere, as long as we can be with him. Good riddance to the rest of it.

Everything we need is here. We have our clothes. Simon has his puzzles and toys, and I have my computers. We won't be here forever, I guess. Just for the rest of my father's life.

>_

I record my father's voice on my phone. Audio, but no video. I'm too worried about the slightness of his arms, the paleness of his skin. I record his voice because his voice still sounds right. He sounds like my father, and it is my father I want to remember.

I record him on every visit. His jokes and laughter. His calm acceptance of death. His puns. The creak in his words when he talks about my little brother, the waif. When he talks about my mother. About me. I have never listened to anything as closely as I listen to these recordings. The ups and downs of tone. The reason for every small inflection. There's so much meaning in every stupid little thing we say.

Sometimes I hold the phone in my hand. Sometimes I set it on the table, or on the bed beside him. So the sound quality varies. It can make him feel far away, when I listen at home. Like his voice is coming to me from behind a thick hanging curtain. But that is only because he's still alive. When he is gone, these recordings will sound closer.

I record everything. Then I copy everything to a laptop that I've spray-painted gold. On the laptop's lid, I've stencilled an old-fashioned cross in white. I know absolutely nothing about religion. This has nothing to do with religion.

I am thorough with my recordings, but organization is a struggle. I divide them into phrases, sentences. Each recording sliced into its parts. Sometimes just single words or sounds. Sometimes just a laugh. I have so many variations of his laugh.

```
quick_laugh.wav

sharp_final_laugh.wav

long_rolling_laughter.wav

longer_laugh_together_mom.wav

sad_laugh.wav

unexpected_laugh.wav

laugh_for_me.wav
```

But the most important thing is my father's voice.
The words.

```
poetic.wav

youre_my_daughter.wav

sunday.wav

sunday_sunday_sunday_monster_truck.wav

birds_and_bees.wav

sleepy_town_blanket.wav

handsome_old.wav

chickens.wav

a_leaf.wav
```

"A weight will lift," he says. "A leaf will fall." I am collecting my father's words. "Fresh white snow will blanket this whole sleepy town."

I built a database to keep track of it all. Every file gets an entry in the database. Each filename was associated with a written transcription and with a text field where I tried to describe the context. But that wasn't enough. So I added text fields for content, for tone, for facial expression. There's so much that needs to be remembered. Bemusement. Mock outrage. Metaphor. It is an unusable mess of data.

At night, I play long nonsense loops of his voice to myself before I fall asleep. Like a bedtime story. Like a lullaby.

>_·

Our room is lousy with flowers. They're on the wall-paper, the ceiling. Carved into the doorframe. They're painted on the too-small chairs set in front of the book-shelf. This whole room feels so strangely lost in time, like an old photograph.

The waif and I share a bunk bed. He prefers the bottom bunk, worried that he might fall in his sleep. But it doesn't matter to me. I don't mind the top bunk. When I am up there, it feels cut off from the room, more private. And I don't care if I fall.

If I had a choice, I'd prefer an actual bed, and my own room. And there are two more bedrooms on this floor, but they're not for us. One is for our uncles, when they arrive; the other is for our mother. This room is ours.

I am a bit too big for the bunk, though. My feet push against the footboard, and there is no room for a computer. Let alone three. That was going to be a problem. So I cleaned out the closet. I made it mine. The door is not soundproof, but it is dark in there, and private, and I even sort of like that I need to hug my knees to my chest to fit. So now, while my brother sleeps, I curl up in front of the machines and upload my father's voice. I make new entries in the database.

"Good morning, Sunday," he says. "How was the flight?"

"Who're you typing to on that thing? A boy? Does he know any knock-knock jokes?"

"How come the cat never comes to visit? Is she mad at me?"

"You are so wonderful, Sunday." His voice is very quiet and serious on that recording. I have a whole special tag for the recordings where he says my name. And for the ones where he says he loves me. Sometimes serious, and sometimes laughing happily.

```
update recordings_db
set tone = 'laughing happily'
where filename = wonderful.wav;
```

"Don't tell your mother or Simon, but I love you *way* more than either of them," he says.

```
update recordings_db
set tone = 'dead serious'
where filename = loves_me_most.wav;
```

The small flowers on the closet's wallpaper flicker with computer light.

>_

There's an abandoned farmhouse across the road from
my grandmother's house. The wood is bleached grey,
and its roof has caved on the right side, like the house
has stumbled to the left. There's no sense of despera-
tion to the house. It doesn't struggle. It doesn't thrash,
or fight against its collapse. It is an elephant that has
come far enough and can go no further. The proud
grey husk of an animal that has earned each crease in
its hide. That has lived long enough. Here is his reward.

It's getting dark now. The sky is the only thing you can see clearly.

I've been sitting and watching. I want to touch the side of that old house. To put my hand on its flank and feel something creak in those big hollow lungs. But when I stand up to walk down there, the dark dissuades me. The sky still has colour, and the stars have begun to show, but the ground and shrubs along my grandmother's driveway are gone. Vanished.

The stumbling old farmhouse is just a silhouette against the stars now. That wouldn't be such a bad way to die. To finally stumble and fall in a field, and to accept it. To be your own gravestone. It would be childish to struggle. Childish to thrash, or fight against your collapse. Childish to try and live forever. I can see my father out in that field, calm and quiet. I am the one still thrashing. I am the one who wants him to live forever.

"Sunday, dear, are you out there?" my grandmother calls from behind me. Inside the orange glow. "Sunday, how much potato salad do you want?" Another late supper. The clatter of cutlery on flowered plates.

Look at that house, so quiet and willing. If there is a good way to die, that's it out there. Graceful and calm in the face of inevitability.

It feels generous, almost. Beauty and reassurances are not for ourselves. Of course death will come. And of course there is no good way to die. There is no peace. A weight will not lift. A leaf will not fall. But we can pretend.

>_

I listen to my father's voice to calm down sometimes. But that is not why I record him.

I record him because I am writing a computer virus. I am writing a computer virus based on my father's words. Based on his jokes and his laughter. Based on his stories. The virus will go out into the world and it will live forever on the hard drives of strangers. It will hide underneath everything, and in the dark it will very quietly repeat things my father has said. Every word that I've recorded.

It won't say anything out loud. It won't speak in his actual voice. Partly because the sound files are too large to include in the virus itself. Partly because his survival will depend on not being heard. Not being discovered. So the virus will say his words for him; it will copy them into memory. Into the long stretches of unused storage. Like an echo in an empty room. Like the words written on the back of an old photograph, hidden by the frame. Like a ghost.

And while the recordings are too large to include in their entirety, his voice does matter. So I messed with the configuration of open source voice recognition software. I set it to analyze file after file after file. To compare and contrast. I fed it laughter. Jokes. I fed it each quiet question, every dry observation. I fed everything through, and the software gave me a short string of digits. Just a fragment of a fingerprint. A pattern.

And that pattern went into the virus source code. Not strictly necessary, but important to me.

His laughter became a part of the pattern the virus used to recognize itself. It became a part of the cryptography the virus used to mutate, to hide my father's plain text quotes from the anti-virus software that might look for him. Everywhere I used it, the pattern decreased the randomness of the virus's behaviour so that, instead of pseudo-randomly choosing which changes it might make on an infected system, it chooses to behave based on this one number. Not for everything, of course. But in some places—in some moments—instead of flipping a coin, the virus will just do what it wants. It will be itself.

This isn't the most efficient way to do this. It isn't the smartest, either.

It feels right, though.

>_

My father has no idea about the virus, mind you. He wouldn't understand a word I told him. Maybe he would understand the basic idea of it, but the basic idea of it is something I tell him every day. I don't want my father to die. He knows. Every day he knows.

Mom is the programmer, not Dad. Yes, Dad's very proud when I win programming competitions, but he just smiles when things get too technical. He never got the hang of computers. Never saw the point. "Look how beautiful it is outside," is what he says. Even on the ugliest days.

Two years ago, when I was suspended from school for hacking, my mother was furious. Not at me, but at the vice-principal who had sent me home. My father and I sat at the kitchen table and listened to her on the phone. Her voice got louder and louder.

"No, I understand exactly what she did," my mom said. "Do you?" She listened. "So let me get this straight. Private emails and data belonging to *my children* and hundreds of other *children* have been needlessly at risk for more than a year because you wanted to save some money running your own servers, and you're suspending my daughter for bringing it to your attention? You don't even have a proper IT person. My daughter was trying to help."

Which wasn't exactly my motivation, if I'm being honest, but it sure sounded good. My father, though, just sat there smiling.

"Some time off school, eh?" he said to me. "That's fun!"

>_

At first, I like the way she dresses. Simple black clothes. Tight black hair. I like it because this is the way I try to dress. It's how I want to see myself. I want to be as unadorned as possible. A cipher. I don't want my clothes to betray anything that is going on inside me. A black hole from which no information should escape.

Her white lab coat is out of place with the rest of her outfit. It is an intentional mistake, almost certainly. Not practical. The lab coat is a concession, the one piece of the doctor costume she wears. A prop. Otherwise, though? Simple. So yes, I like the way she dresses. But it's hard to like someone whose job is to treat you like a child.

She's a psychiatrist, I've figured out. She hasn't told me that, yet. She just leads the way. Down one long wide hospital hallway after another. She doesn't say where we're going, either, but there are coloured stripes on the floor. They go different ways. Colours come and colours go, but there's one that is always under our feet. Blue, which a legend on the wall decodes for me as "pediatric psychiatry."

Our destination is a room clearly meant for children. Children-children, I mean. Waif-aged things. But here I am, so I guess it is meant for me, too. There's apparently no institutional distinction between me and the waif. Two peas in a pod, even though he is half my age.

Still, there's enough of a distinction between me and my brother that they decided to deal with us separately. He's back in the hospital room, waiting his turn. The doctor pulls out a chair for me and one for herself.

There are plush creatures everywhere, a soft alligator, fuzzy and dark green, a hippo drooping across a box of latex gloves, a stuffed eagle with her wings outstretched and her beak felted.

"I've been asked to help you prepare," the doctor says. I don't need this. I know that my father is dying, and I know what I have to do. The waif should be the one here. He would fit right in. I can picture him hugging an adorable raptor, his expression blank as ever.

We're back in the city for a scan they can only do at a real hospital. Nobody has their hopes up. I wonder if this doctor is my mother's idea. But that's ungenerous of me. My mother isn't spiteful. And she isn't cheesy, either. My mother is better than this.

The doctor talks and talks. She does not talk nearly as efficiently as she dresses.

People are so repetitive. Why? The way they talk is useless. All of the information is front-loaded in the context and in those first few words. The rest is repetition, redundancy, emphasis. A waste of time. This is just how everyone talks now. Listen to them. Are all conversations supposed to be like this? For the rest of my life? I hate it.

And look at these toys. None of these creatures are soft in the real world. Perversions of danger, twisted, adorable shadows of death, made huggable. Blanketed in snow.

"A weight will lift," I feel like saying.

"Your father is going to die. He's very afraid," the doctor says.

And then she says it for another half an hour.

>_

In the hallway, I play back part of the recording.

"Your father is going to die. He's very afraid," the doctor says.

This is a waste of my phone's memory. I delete every moment of her.

She is gone forever.

>_

When I come in, there's no time for a joke about the stuffed animals. My mother is already standing, and she hugs me before I can say a word. I hug her back, forgetting my carefully worded joke. I squeeze her tight, because it is unexpected. Because it is warm and I love her, and because she does not ever hug us. No matter how tight I squeeze, though, she's squeezing tighter. It is very difficult to not start crying.

I can't look at my dad yet. Instead, I look over my

mother's shoulder to Simon. He's staring at us with no expression at all.

Behind us, the doctor appears again. All in black, nothing like me at all. Knocking on the door with the same fake-tentative knock she used on her first visit. My mother lets me go and takes the waif by the hand.

"Hello, Simon," the doctor says to him. She turns and leads the way. My mother and brother disappear down the hall, following the blue line on the floor. Their turn in the declawed raptor sanctuary.

My father has books piled up on his nightstand. Paperbacks and hardcovers. Library books and brand new purchases. Thrillers. Tough, ruthless, cold-hearted men of action who nonetheless do the right thing in the end. I've tried to read them. I really tried. It could have been something to share with him. They aren't for me, though. They feel empty.

My father has a weakness for them. His word, weakness. Weakness doesn't seem quite correct, though.

A weakness for having no weaknesses at all? A soft

spot for violence and happy endings. A weakness for everything turning out right every time. After the twist, of course. A soft spot for the twist.

"How did it go?" my father asks.

I am still a bit shaky from my mother's hug. And the books seem like a perfect distraction. I point at them.

"Really?" I say. "More?"

He shrugs.

"Dying doesn't cure boredom," he says. He's still looking at me, wondering about the psychiatrist.

"They told me you're going to die, and that you're very afraid," I tell him. "They told me I have to be brave for both of us."

"Like on TV?" my father says.

"Like on TV," I say. I love his smile.

>_

Something has been growing behind my father's pain and behind my father's jokes these last days of his life. It isn't the fear I was instructed to expect. That is there, of course. There are moments when my father looks afraid. Always when my mother is here, like he's afraid for her benefit. Or maybe he is strong for mine. But that isn't what I mean. That isn't what I see growing behind his eyes. And it isn't bravery, either. It is something else entirely. A calmness and a confidence have put down roots in him.

I shouldn't say "these last few days of his life." My mother tenses up when I say things like that in front of Simon. When I get too close to an honest assessment. I have to talk the way she talks, for the waif's benefit. I have to be careful. Never lie, but don't let the truth slip out. He'll melt if the truth touches him. So hope springs eternal, in my brother's presence. There is always hope. Without hope we are lost. Hope is a shining light in the darkness of what is actually happening, and as long as we can keep my younger brother well lit, nothing bad will ever happen and everything will turn out alright in the end.

"Are you going to die?" the waif asks my father today. Nobody has told me how his session with the psychiatrist went.

"We don't know for sure," my mother says, even though we do. We do know for sure.

"Hope springs eternal," I say gravely.

My mother gives me a dangerous look. I look right back at her.

"What does that mean?" My brother is looking at me now, confused.

"Without hope we are lost," I say. "There is always hope. Hope is the shining light in the deepest darkness." I try to keep my face deadly serious, the way my father does.

"Sunday," my mother warns.

The waif is so confused that he starts crying.

>_

I have all three computers set up in my closet now, constantly running. My grandmother found me a long orange extension cord, and I made my mother buy me a power bar in Truro. Enough to handle the power adapters for all three. To handle my external hard drive. I found an old nightstand in the attic. One computer sits underneath, with just enough space for the cover to stay open. The other sits open on top. The third sits on my lap when I'm here. On the floor when I am not.

"Good lord," my grandmother said when she saw

the cords coiled everywhere, the laptops open and flickering, one above the other. "Don't get those wrapped around your neck! You'll strangle."

Which seems like an insane thing to say.

Simon is off on his own again.

This whirring, overheated little room is mine and mine alone.

Two of the laptops are disconnected from the internet but connected to one another. Each is running a different operating system, for testing purposes. I chose common but slightly out-of-date versions of the most popular operating systems. Vulnerable but everywhere.

This is where my father's ghost waits.

He is not ready yet. One computer infects the other, sometimes, with his memory. He slips between them, back and forth. But only imperfectly. And not as frequently as he should. It only works sometimes, and I don't yet know why.

And if it only works sometimes here—on a system I control, with software that I know and understand— how can I expect him to survive out in the world, with dozens of operating systems? Millions of combinations of software and hardware! No. It's not ready yet. Not resilient enough. I need to find a better selection of vulnerabilities to exploit. A stronger suite of infection vectors. I need backup exploits, too, ways for the virus to spread if the first method fails.

I have been focused too much on his words. I've been neglecting the code itself. The virus part of this virus. But the words are important. My living father still has more to say. I want as many of his jokes and kindnesses to make it into the software as possible, before I introduce him to that third computer, stencilled grey and black with a half-joking Ouija board.

When everything is ready, it won't matter how beautiful a day it is outside. I am going to summon the dead.

>_

We say our goodbyes for the night. Crowded beside his hospital bed. Every night we pretend to be casual. We pretend we aren't being careful. Careful to ensure that our goodnights will be adequate if this turns out to be the real goodnight. If tonight's the night.

"Give Daddy one more kiss, Simon. Say you love him."

"I love you, Daddy."

"Say, 'See you tomorrow, Daddy.'"

"See you tomorrow, Daddy."

They go out the door first and I linger in the doorway for just a moment, phone in hand.

"Goodbye forever," I say. Our secret nightly ritual.

"Goodbye forever," he says.

-- TWO --

>_

"Goodbye forever" is the perfect joke, because forever is impossible.

Every night I say it, and every morning I see my father again. Forever is meaningless. Tough talk, an empty threat. Forever is our secret handshake. Our code word. Our decoder ring. Not a measurement of time at all. I know this because "Goodbye forever" comes easy. The passage of actual time is much more difficult.

After we leave the hospital, the hours and the minutes just stretch and stretch. They pull nothing from all four corners, 'til it blankets and smothers every night with its emptiness. Still, time is not my enemy. I have my recordings, and I have a virus to construct.

I squirrel up in this closet with these laptops and their unnatural light, listening to the day's sound files, copying out words and phrases. Sometimes whole sentences, if they feel right.

I work on improving the code itself, too, sometimes, but just as often that part of the virus sits neglected while I obsess over the selection of my father's words.

```
update recordings_db
set transcription = 'goodbye forever'
where filename = say_goodbye.wav;
```

I will put "Goodbye forever" into the virus, but it will be the very last thing. The finishing touch. There is so much more to say before goodbye.

My dad was in a good mood today. He and my mom laughed a lot, the way they used to, teasing each other with in-jokes that I'll never get. Memories of people and places outside my frame of reference. A life they got to share together. I can almost see all of that information, like a database of facts and moments that I do not have access to. Like a book on a shelf that I can't quite reach, and my mother and father keep quoting from it and laughing. It's a book they read together.

There's so much I don't know how to transcribe. I wish I could encode that feeling from his words. That implied shared history. The warmth and affection. This plain text is just a skeleton.

>_

I've started a playlist of my dad's dumb jokes about dying. There's a light in my father's voice when he jokes like this, that he knows will brighten the room.

"Dying *and* handsome. Mothers, lock up your daughters!"

"They better not have chickens in heaven. Chickens are idiot eagles, and I hate them."

"Nurse, could you have the doctors check to make sure I have the right skeleton in? This doesn't feel like mine."

"Hmmmm. What should I wear today?"

"Dying isn't even the worst part of all this. The worst part is that I'll never get to be a cranky old lady in line at the grocery store."

"Oh good. We all lived another day. I mean, some of us had to work harder at it than others. I'm just saying."

"I'm not kidding. Chickens are garbage."

"Was that a smile? You can't laugh at my jokes, I'm dying!"

and,

"To be honest, I feel kind of foolish for eating all those salads."

I like to lay in the top bunk at night and stare at the weird uneven stucco faces in the ceiling. And I drift off to the sound of my father not being afraid.

>_

Our mother has never really acknowledged that he's dying. She knows just as well as we do. Better, probably. Yet she's never actually said the words in front of us. I've been assuming that this is to protect Simon, although, of course, she uses the same careful language with me. We're both her children. We both need to be protected. It must have been hard for her to let that doctor speak so bluntly. "Your father is going to die." Did the doctor say it just like that to the waif, too? I can imagine the colour draining out of my mother's face at those words. We both need to be protected, but Simon especially. Simon is . . . delicate.

Since that day, things feel different. She never lied to us before. But she was very careful to tiptoe around the truth. Lately, she seems less careful. Today, for instance.

"We're going to buy your father one last steak before he dies," she announces at the breakfast table. "And we're going to have one last movie night, all of us together, like we used to. Your father deserves a treat."

And so, after cereal, we climb into the car together, and we drive all the way to Halifax to buy our father his last steak.

"His favourite," Mom explains as we drive, "is the Del Monico 7 oz. Derby style from the Steak and Stein. Medium," she says. "Not a fancy steak. Not a fifty-dollar filet mignon from the Keg Mansion, prepared ice blue. Nope. Just a cheap steak drowned in marinade; we used to eat them all the time."

When we get there, she tells the waiter the same thing.

"This might be the last steak he ever eats," she tells him. "He loved eating here." The waiter looks understanding, but a bit nervous, too. We order four steak dinners to go, and, when they come, we pile back into the car and drive an hour and a half back to Tatamagouche to the care centre where my father does not suspect a thing.

Our mother holds the to-go bags behind her back.

"What have you got there?" he says.

And his face lights up when he sees those Steak and Stein bags. Beside me, Simon is carrying an armload of dishes we borrowed from our grandmother's kitchen. He sets them down on the bed, excitedly.

"It might be the last steak you'll ever eat!" my little brother says.

>_

"We're going to have a movie night," my mother says as she's packing our garbage into Steak and Stein bags. My father has hardly touched his meal. He can't keep solid food down this week. But he smiles as she takes it from his tray. "Family movie night," my mother says. "The way we used to." Beside her, Simon nods very seriously.

"One last movie night," my brother says, and my mother throws the garbage into the bin harder than she intended.

"Simon, what did I *just* tell you?" she says. But my father is laughing.

"One last movie night sounds wonderful, Simon," he says. "What are we going to watch?"

"Anything you want," I say. I pull my laptop out of my bag. "You name it, and I can get it for us."

For his last movie, my father requests the black-and-white 1950 film *Harvey*, starring Jimmy Stewart. He asks me to look up the old posters, too, with Jimmy Stewart and a big rabbit shadow. To download pictures from the original stage play, which was written by Mary Chase. To find a copy of the trailer for us to watch. Coming soon!

"I can do that," I tell him.

"Does your last movie have to be black-and-white?" Simon says.

"It isn't *my* last movie," my father says. "It's *our* last movie. And *Harvey* is the best movie ever made, Simon. I want to watch it with you."

By the time I've downloaded the movie, they've piled the bed high with borrowed pillows. The harsh fluorescent lights are all turned off, and my mother has plugged in a soft yellow lamp borrowed from our grandmother's house. They're all waiting for me, crowded around my father in the quiet room. It really does feel like movie night. The waif even has a bowl of burnt popcorn, from the nurses' break room.

For the whole movie, my father taps his hand on me or my brother whenever a good line is coming up. He holds his breath at the exciting parts. He laughs too loud and looks to make sure that we're laughing, too. He squeezes my hand while Jimmy Stewart gives a little speech. Two separate times, I look over and catch him with tears on his cheeks and shining eyes. Then he's laughing and looking at me again.

He slips back and forth like that, one moment completely lost in the world of the movie, and then suddenly and obviously excited that we're here watching with him. Afterwards, he quotes his favourite lines, doing a bad Jimmy Stewart impression. His voice lilting like crazy into the high-torn registers. But the impression isn't the point. He's in love with the words themselves. The ideas. I record all of it on my phone.

Jimmy Stewart's character in the film is named Elwood P. Dowd, and the quote I like best is this one, in my father's voice:

"Years ago, my mother used to say to me, she'd say, 'In this world, Elwood, you must be,'—she always called me Elwood—'In this world, Elwood, you must be oh so smart or oh so pleasant.' Well, for years I was smart."

My father pauses for effect.

"I recommend pleasant. You may quote me."

Over the next few hours, he quotes that line again and again, and every time he says it he includes the "you may quote me" at the end, even though it obviously isn't the important part.

When I get home, I transcribe the recordings into the virus. It is so confusing. Is this really him? He's saying someone else's words. Mary Chase's words, in Jimmy Stewart's voice, but they so clearly mean something to him. He says them like he's thankful that someone finally gave him words for things he's always wanted to say. He believes those words. You can hear it in his voice. You could see it on his face. And if words mean something to you, if an idea moves you, aren't you changed, just a little?

>_

Dad is on a roll, telling stupid jokes one after the other while Simon sits on the hospital bed grinning from ear to ear. I would stay here forever, if I could. Not saying a word, just listening. Recording. I don't even mind the sound of the crushed ice in his plastic cup. This is as close to perfect as we're ever going to get.

My mother, on the other hand, is agitated because she and I haven't eaten. She's standing by the door now. When the nurse brought Dad his lunch, she brought an extra tray for Simon, so they've both eaten. We have not. You have to eat every day so that you can live until the next day. Then you have to eat again the next day. Food is an inconvenience. A hassle. What is the good of medical science if we still have to interrupt whatever we're doing to eat three times a day? There should just be a pill you can take.

"We have to go, Sunday," my mother says.

I don't want to miss anything. This is all important. Every stupid word. But I can't tell her that. Not without telling her that I am recording this all on my phone. Without having to explain why. Without giving away my plan. So we have to go.

We have to go and the waif can stay. The waif will get to hear these jokes, get to spend these moments with our father that I won't get. These jokes could all be in the virus. They could live on forever. But instead Simon is the only one who will ever hear them.

"Sunday, now," my mother says.

"I know," I say, trying to keep the irritation out of my voice. I shouldn't be mad at the waif. It isn't his fault that he's useless. And anyway, it's hard to be mad at somebody who looks so genuinely happy.

I casually set my phone on the side table, behind Dad's books. It is still recording. I hope that the battery lasts.

"Pick Simon up some mints," Dad says.

"I don't enjoy mints very much," my brother tells him.

"Pick Simon up some mints, and I'll eat them."

And then we go, leaving the two of them alone.

>_

I'm trying to be as quiet as possible, trying not to wake my brother. But the whole bunk bed creaks and groans every time I move. When I reach the bottom of the ladder, I am genuinely surprised to find him still asleep. He looks nervous, even when he's unconscious. His brow slightly furrowed. His hand up to his mouth, muscle memory from when he used to suck his thumb. The waif in his purest form.

I cross the room and curl into my spot in the closet. I was worried all day yesterday. Worried that one of them would find the phone, would see that it was recording. And I was worried that I had crossed a line. That I was violating their privacy. Now, though, listening to the recording, I regret nothing.

There are some good jokes, and I am glad I didn't miss them. Phrases and words that will be perfect to copy into the virus. But there's something else here, too. Something new. A conversation I never would have heard otherwise.

"Hey, now," my father says on the recording. "Why are you crying?"

There's no answer. Just more crying, and my father murmuring reassuring words that I can't make out. Then Simon says something, too quiet and garbled to understand. I can hear the tears in his voice, even if I have no idea what he's saying.

"Simon, I have no idea what you just said," my father says. But he says it gently.

"I don't want you to die," Simon says, louder. He's still crying.

Of course Simon doesn't want our father to die. I

don't know why it is so unexpected for me to hear him say the words. But it is. Did I think that my brother was crying all the time just because he's a baby? Just because he's a delicate flower? Over in his bunk, Simon is still sleeping.

"I don't want you to die," he says again on the recording, even louder now. Defiant.

>_

I don't want my father to die. He knows. Every day I don't want him to die, and every day he knows.

Simon doesn't want him to die, either.

"I know, Simon," my father says on the recording, more gently than he says those words to me. Or maybe he's just being gentle in a different way.

I don't know how I will transcribe any of this. The way he sounds, talking to my little brother, is different from how he sounds when talking just to me. I feel certain that it means something different, too, even though the words are the exact same. This particular softness in my father's voice is meant only for Simon.

There are parts of my father that he shows only to Simon. Parts he shows only to my mother. What if I had never heard this? What if I had never realized this? Would this whole virus have been made up only of who my father was to me?

I thought this was going to be easy. I would write down my father's words, and he would live forever. But the more I record, the more I realize I am missing.

So no, I don't regret recording them in secret. I have to record everything. I have to record him when he is with Simon. When he's with my mom. I need to find a way into his computer. Into his emails. His old pictures. I have to save as much of him as I can. Not just the part I can see with my own two eyes. Because now that I have started, it's up to me how much of my father survives.

I know that this computer virus will never *actually* be my father. It is a few lines of computer code, a text file filled with bad jokes. I know that it can't replace the incomprehensible mess of human life. But it can be *something*. I have to believe that it can be something.

>_

Our mother waves once as she climbs into her car. She starts the engine and pulls around the driveway loop heading up the gravel toward the road. She looks distracted, as she passes us. Unhappy. My little brother, though, keeps right on waving until she's gone. It is one and a half hours to the airport from here. She's going to pick up Uncle Frank and Uncle Jonah and bring them back here. Our job, in her absence, is to prepare their room. Back inside the house, our grandmother is baking macaroni and cheese.

"Do you know where the extra quilts are?" she asks as we pass.

We do.

Upstairs, we open the extra room. Simon has an armload of bedding, and I've got the cleaning supplies. The wallpaper is less flowery than in ours. Just a simple pattern of browns faded together. It matches the heavy wooden furniture. Only the chair by the window seems delicate, upholstered with a faded green flower print, but even that feels more serious than the flowers in our bedroom. We prop open the window to let in the fresh afternoon air. We dust and vacuum. We change the bedsheets, spread out the comforter and quilt.

And when we're done, Simon sits on the edge of the big bed.

"This room is nicer," my brother says. "But I like our bunk beds."

I don't say anything. I don't have an opinion. I'm just glad to be done, so I can get back to my computers. Simon follows me, the way he always does, and he watches me curl into my small space in the closet. I reach out to close the door, but then catch myself. It usually bothers me, the way the waif is always watching. But I'm starting to think that's because I'm selfish. I spend so much time worrying about myself, my own plans and thoughts, that I don't even really see my brother.

Instead of closing the closet door, I wave him closer.

He takes a step and then pauses.

"It's okay," he says. "I can leave you alone."

I lift up my headphones and hold one of the earbuds out. The cord stretches far enough for him to put one in his ear and me to put one in mine. I watch patiently as he figures out how it fits. On my main laptop, I find one of the long sound files I've made of our father's voice. This one isn't jokes or movie quotes. It isn't declarations of love or fear or sadness. It's my father asking what lunch will be, what time it is. My father saying, "Oh yeah," and, "I was wondering."

Simon sits closer on the carpet beside me, and I play it for him.

>_

Simon and I sit together, listening to Dad's voice. My brother doesn't say anything, he just listens and fiddles with the headphone cord. I am trying not to stare, but it's hard. My father will say something, and my own emotions will play across my brother's face. Dad will say a word just slightly wrong, and my own confusion will furrow Simon's brow. He keeps squeezing my hand. Or I keep squeezing his. I want to ask him questions. What does he think of this? Does he understand? But

<69>

I don't say anything. I don't want to ruin this moment, whatever it is.

But it turns out the moment is over anyway.

"Bunk beds! Well, aren't you lucky! I've been trying to convince Jonah for *years* to get bunk beds." Uncle Frank is here, leaning in from the hallway, his hand on the door frame. Simon and I scramble to our feet, headphones out. I close the laptop.

"Uncle Frank!" the waif says. Frank is our father's brother.

"What on earth are you doing in the closet?" Frank is big and seems even bigger when he lifts me up in a hug. It feels immediately familiar to be hugged by him, even though we haven't seen him in more than a year. I hug him back, tight. He even smells the same, like perfumed pine needles. He's the only person I know who wears cologne, and it is everywhere. In his beard and thick knit sweater. In his hair. I can still smell it after he lets me go. "Aren't you a sight for sore eyes," he says to me, his hand still on my shoulder.

"I'm a sight for sore eyes, too!" my brother says,

and Frank laughs. He pulls Simon into a hug, lifting my little brother up off the floor and spinning him around. I can't remember the last time I heard Simon giggle. It's a ridiculous sound—exactly the sound you would expect someone so small and frail to make. Frank sets him down, and the waif stands there, startled and delighted at the same time. "You're here!" he says.

"You didn't know we were coming?"

"I did!"

Our uncle Jonah is here, too, setting the last of their suitcases on the floor, leaning an umbrella against the doorframe.

He looks tired from their flight, but he's smiling. His smiles are much smaller than his husband's, more restrained but just as genuine. The two of them have been together since before Simon was born. He reaches out to shake my hand. "Sunday," he says. "You look well." He has a Haitian accent and a good handshake. He doesn't talk slowly, but he speaks more carefully than Frank does. He does everything more carefully than Frank.

He shakes Simon's hand, too.

"You are much bigger, Simon," he says.

"I'm a sight for sore eyes," my brother says.

"Yes, you are," Jonah says. Then to Frank, "We should get settled in."

"Okay. Okay. Okay." Frank grins at us and picks up a bag. "I still think we should get bunk beds," he says to his husband as they disappear into their room. Simon and I stand in our doorway, listening to them talk. "I mean, really, separate bedrooms would be perfect," Uncle Frank continues. "But even bunk beds would be nice. Up high above the room, with some space all to myself when I need it. Or when you need it. Not every night. Obviously. But it would be reassuring somehow, right? A place to hibernate."

"If you say so."

"It saved my Aunt Edie and Uncle Harry's marriage, you know. They had separate cabins," Frank says. "Right next door to each other. And they stayed married for fifty years."

"I know that," Jonah says. "Do you want to know how I know that? I know because you pointed it out on the drive up here, less than one hour ago. You point it out every time we drive up here."

Downstairs, my mother is calling for them.

"Hurry up," she yells. "Visiting hours are only 'til five today."

They're here to see my father while they still can. To say goodbye, same as us.

>_

"I'm the only one who ever cries," Simon says to my father on that recording, when nobody else was there to hear. "Sunday never cries. Mom never cries. Just me." Which isn't true, of course. If anything, I cry too much. I just never let the waif see me cry.

I keep listening to this conversation. I should be transcribing new sections, or working on finding a more reliable exploit for the virus to use. But I keep coming back to listen to this awkward private conversation, where my brother sounds more like a real person than I've ever heard him sound. He has always been the waif to me. Too delicate. Weak and frail. A punchline more than a person. I love him, but I am starting to realize that I don't really see him.

I don't really see my father, either. Or my mother. The whole world has been revolving around me for as long as I can remember. I feel like someone just threw cold water on me. I'm awake now. I'm all wet.

I'm so stupid.

"I miss when Sunday and I were friends," my brother says, at the end of the recording. And that made me feel bad in a way I can't even describe.

>_

For the past few nights, after everyone's gone to bed and it's just me and Simon, I've been talking to him more. Not about anything important, really. I don't think I could talk to him about Dad. Or about our mother. But we've been talking. I've been trying to explain computer programming to him, and he seems interested. We lie in the dark, and he asks question after question until one of us falls asleep. And then the next night it picks up, right from where we stopped.

"What are the Boolean operators again?" he says.

"You know this one already."

"I don't remember them."

"Well, which ones do you remember?" I ask him.

And he lists them for me. NAND, AND, OR, XOR. He learns faster than I do.

"What is XOR?" I say, because that's the one he forgot last night.

"Exclusive OR," the waif says. "One of the two values has to be true, but the other one has to be false."

"And what is NOR?"

"Not OR," he says. We talk like this for an hour, maybe. Every night. He asks his quiet questions about computers and I try to answer the best I can. He makes me promise him again tonight that I will show him how to write a computer program. A calculator program is what we decided on. Something simple, but not too simple. He asks me about the different programming languages we might use. Which ones do I like the best? Why? Eventually, his voice starts drifting away while he talks. Drifting in and out of focus. Either he's falling asleep, or I am.

There's a long pause where nobody talks at all, and it feels like the night is over. But then he says one last thing.

"Thank you for talking to me."

>_

There's no moon tonight. None of the windows in the back of the house are lit. So while I know the pond is there, I can see only the faint shape where the water reflects the sky, where the yard is wearing two different shades of black. I came down here to be alone, but this is not the kind of alone I wanted. Nothing out here seems comforting. It's just empty.

Turn the corner, though, and noise is everywhere. A house filled with family, gathered around the kitchen table. It lights the whole driveway, the red gravel loop around the big trees. The tire swing that hangs there. I sit down on the step, with my back to the front door. The clatter of dishes and laughter. Uncles, grandmother, family. This is better. Being alone is more satisfying when there's a crowd nearby.

Even the sky seems lighter in this direction. The field out there isn't black on black; it has a texture and shape. There are streaks of grey cloud and blank sky. I can see the outline of that old elephant of a house, still stumbling in its field. I can make out the window and the small front door. My father's calm is still there in that field, in the shape of the house, in the dark eye of the window. I wish I could get my fingers around that calm somehow. It would soak up this childish anger.

"We've gone over this," my father said today. There was none of that Simon-gentleness in his voice. I told him again that I didn't want him to die. I said every single thing I knew I shouldn't say.

"Why aren't you fighting this?" I said. "Why are you just lying there, dying? I heard the doctor. You could have done another round of chemotherapy."

"Sunday, it isn't that simple," he said.

"Don't you care about us at all?" I said.

I haven't transcribed the recording, yet. I don't want to transcribe it. I'm ashamed.

>_

Downstairs, Frank is telling a story too loudly.

"We rode that bike right down the side of the mountain; there was no path."

"There was a path," Uncle Jonah says. "There most certainly was a path. You just thought you knew better."

"Frank always knows better," my mother laughs. "That doesn't seem to help much, does it, Frank?"

"Anyway," Jonah sounds tired, "maybe we should stop the story here and prepare for bed. We should stop now while everybody still respects—"

"We shat blood," Frank interrupts him. "Or anyway, I shat blood." My mother's laughter again, and my grandmother's disapproving clicking. "I thought I was going to have to go to the hospital for sure," Frank says.

Beside me, on the stairs, Simon is laughing as quietly as he can. He was already here when I came inside the house. Grinning from ear to ear. So I sat down and joined him. We've been sitting here for an hour now, just listening to our mother and our uncles drink their wine and tell stories.

"Don't show off," Jonah says. "It was hardly any blood."

"I shat blood!"

"Having blood in your shit, that's different from shitting blood," Jonah's voice again.

"Oh really? Thank you, Doctor Science." They're both so deadpan, like comedians who've performed together for years. They have a comfortable rhythm.

"In any case," Jonah says, "you made your bed, isn't that how the expression goes?"

The briefest pause and then:

"I shat my bed, you mean." Everyone is laughing, chairs scrape against the tile floor of the kitchen. A bottle clinks against a glass.

"At least it was your own bed," my mother says, after a moment. "Some of us were not so lucky."

"Now *that* sounds like a story I desperately want to hear," Frank says. More laughter. "Regale us with the shameful horrors of your youth!"

Simon leans his head on my shoulder, and together we sit on the stairs and we listen.

>_

"What does it copy?" The waif is asking questions in the dark again, but I can't remember where we left off last night. The room feels too warm. This whole house is always so warm, even when there's no fire in the kitchen stove.

"What does what copy?"

"The virus," he says. His bunk creaks. "You said it makes copies. What does it make copies of?"

I don't remember any of this. Did I tell Simon about the virus I'm writing? That seems impossible.

I have no plans to tell anyone. Telling Simon would have been a big decision, not one I would forget. Did I talk in my sleep, then? Am I a sleep-talker? How would I even know? I used to sleep alone.

"What virus?" I say.

"You were telling me about computer viruses. Like the ambulance virus that draws an ambulance driving across the screen and it crashes into the side. And the siren plays. Or the plane that flies across the top. You said they make copies, but that was the last thing I remember. I think I fell asleep."

I like this new sound in Simon's voice. This new confidence he has when we're talking. It used to annoy me the way he sounded so unsure of himself all the time. It never occurred to me that maybe he sounded unsure of himself because I never wanted to talk. I was always on my way to do something else. Focused on something that really mattered. Why wouldn't he sound uncertain?

Now, though, he is just talking. The words seem to come out easily. It's a small thing, but one that makes me happy.

"They make a copy of themselves," I tell him. "That's how they spread. They make a copy of themselves and put that copy inside another program on the computer. And then, when somebody runs that newly infected program, the virus runs again, and it makes another copy of itself somewhere. It goes through every email address it can find on the computer and sends a copy of itself to everyone, disguised as some normal file they might click on. It looks for other computers on the local network, or for external storage plugged in to the USB ports. It tries to copy itself to each of these in turn. And so on forever."

This is how I've chosen to spread the virus, in any case. The methods I've settled on. The code I've written.

"Oh. That makes sense." He sounds sleepy already. There's a long silence, where I don't know what to say. I want to keep talking about viruses, to tell him more. I want to describe my old favourites. Or tell him stories of the people who created them. A ghost story before bed, about long-dead pirates. VX writers. Phone phreaks. Hackers.

I want to indoctrinate my brother with the teachings of the Cult of the Dead Cow. Horrify him with tales of the Phone Losers of America. Buy him his very own cereal box replica whistle that blows at 2600 Hz.

I've never met those people, and I probably never will. They wrote their stories and created their viruses before I was born. They're all gone now, replaced by faceless communication security companies who tell no jokes. Who play no pranks. Atlantis sank into the sea, and they built an oil rig where it stood. There are whole majestic libraries down there, filled with dead jokes. An ambulance that drones across the screen to crash into the side wall of a monitor. A blocky, misshapen pixel parachutist. The AIDS virus now infecting your *personal computer*. An elaborate series of pranks and battle cries. An escape from high school or your mindless office job. A type of poetry for the sort of people poetry never wanted.

My people.

I want to say all this, but the waif is quiet now and probably asleep.

The other night, Simon thanked me for talking to him. But I am starting to realize how long it's been since I had someone to talk to, too.

-- THREE --

>_

We're always bringing him something. Cluttering up our father's room. A book for his stack of thrillers. A light summer quilt for when the nights turn cold. A deck of playing cards, which go into the drawer beside the other deck of playing cards we forgot about. There are only so many practical things a person needs. But we still need to bring him things. A glow-stick headband for some silly pictures. A bobble-head doll of a lobster, which is stupid. But stupid is good. Stupid can win a smile.

Today we bring a chessboard that Simon found in an old trunk. A ziplock baggie of little plastic chess pieces. My brother holds them up for our father to see.

"Nice," he says. "Are you going to teach me how to play chess?"

"No!" My brother laughs.

"I told Simon that you'd show him how to play," my mother says.

"And so the blind shall lead the blind," my father says. To Simon, he says, "I would be very happy to teach you how to play chess."

"Don't take your jacket off," my mom says to Simon. She puts the chessboard on the bed beside my dad, and she kisses his cheek. Her jacket is still on, too. "Want anything in particular?" she asks my dad.

"Maybe a hot chocolate today, instead of coffee?" he says.

"Okay," she says. "See you in an hour!" She takes Simon's hand, and they leave.

Every day, my mother and Simon walk to a coffee shop in town, ostensibly for breakfast snacks but really for the fresh air and exercise. For the quiet. Even yesterday, in the pouring rain, they walked.

"That's what raincoats are for," my mother said in response to the waif's complaints.

It's a half hour walk, each way, just for coffee. It seems silly, especially since we drive right past that place every morning. We could easily stop then. From a conservation of effort perspective, it doesn't make any sense at all. It is inefficient, and I prefer to be efficient. Especially now. It seems wrong to spend a half hour walking someplace when we have so little time left with my father. That's an hour lost forever. But if we are being honest, I also don't care much for being outside.

My mother is different. She needs to be outside. She needs to do things. To go places. To talk to people. It drives her crazy to spend the whole day cooped up.

For the first couple weeks, we did things the efficient way. We stopped to pick up snacks on the way to the hospital and stayed the whole day with my father. And at the end of every day, my mother was worn out. She was tired and irritated and sad. Which, of course, could be because we're here every day, sitting around a hospital bed, waiting for her husband to die. But my mom didn't believe that was it. Not entirely.

So she made a change. She started walking, every day. Even when she clearly doesn't feel like it. In the mornings, they walk, and get rained on, and get red mud all over their shoes. They buy scones and coffee, and they come back smiling. At the end of the day, she's not quite as sad, and not quite as tired.

It is logical in a way that makes me jealous, actually. My mother knows herself. She's like a mechanic who can tell what's wrong with a car just by the sounds the engine makes. She can fix things when they go wrong.

>_

While my mother and brother are on their morning walk, my father and I go through the obituaries. We take turns reading them out loud. The language is so boring and repetitive. You see the exact same phrases so many times. Words that were clearly meant to be respectful and traditional come across as formulaic and stupid. "So-and-so will be sorely missed" might be true, but it also sounds like your loved ones copied your obituary word for word from someone who died yesterday.

"They might as well just write, 'This is an obituary,'" my dad says.

"This is an obituary," I say. "These are the words you put in an obituary. Thank you for taking the time to read my obituary."

There is nothing about actual people in any of these memorial postings. There are no mistakes, no great regrets, no broken promises, no stupidities. There are no triumphs. No shining moments of pride, no redemption, no happiness. The language is identical for everyone, filled in with the applicable figures. Age. Number of children. Facts. It's like reading out loud from a database and trying to imagine a real human being from just the numbers.

You could actually write a computer program to generate these, and nobody would ever know the difference. An eighty-nine-year-old woman, survived by a husband, three children, and four grandkids? No problem.

```
my @entire_human_life = ('89', 'F', 'Stroke',
'husband', '3', '4');
```

"Goddamn it," my dad says today. He points to a name. It is a short obituary. Even more clichés than usual. After a long battle with cancer, passed away in his sleep, surrounded by loved ones, etc. Aggressively standard. The kind of obituary that we love to make fun of.

"Surrounded by nameless loved ones," I say, but my father's smile is gone.

"I went to high school with him," he says. "We were best friends." My father rereads the obituary. "Long battle with cancer," he says. "Ugh." He tosses the newspaper onto his side table in disgust, and just like that our game is over.

"I meant to call him," my dad says.

I don't know what to say. I don't want to say "I'm sorry" or any other empty condolences. We spend every morning making fun of all that. But it seems like I should say something. I guess that's where clichés come from, isn't it? Too many people say something just so they can say something. Because they feel like they should. But when there's really nothing to say, anything will sound empty. My father is sad about an old friendship he lost. That's something worth being sad about. So I'm quiet. We sit in silence, and my father looks out the window.

Eventually, though, he remembers that I'm here. He turns back to smile at me. He picks up the obituaries again.

"Okay, who's next?" he says.

"We don't have to."

"Don't be stupid," he says. "Of course we have to. This is research for when you write my obituary. Who else could I trust with this? Sunday, I am counting on you to not let anyone say that I died surrounded by nameless loved ones. Or that I lost my courageous battle with cancer."

"I'll tell people you won," I promise him.

"Exactly!" He laughs. I love it when my father laughs. "You tell people that. The cancer is dead. I did what needed to be done. I'm a hero."

>_

In the car, my mother plays the familiar game of What's Wrong with the Waif, while she drives.

"Are you feeling sick?"

"Are you angry about something?"

"What is it, Simon?"

"Did your father say something that upset you?"

"Did your sister say something?"

Meanwhile, Simon is sitting beside me in silence, just staring out the window. He's been quieter than usual, his hands in fists, and when he went to the bathroom earlier, he slammed the door. Well, his version of slamming a door, anyway. He closed it abruptly, rather than his usual method of carefully turning the knob and gently returning the door to the closed position. Still, I can't really blame my mother for just now noticing. Simon throws tantrums with the volume turned way down. Now that she has noticed, though, she won't let it go.

"Did something happen?"

"Do you think we've been treating you too much like a child?"

"What is it, Simon?"

She never asks the real questions, like, "Is it about your father dying?" "Are you sad that your father is dying?" or "Are you angry that your father is dying?"

Which is fair, because why ask a question when you already know the answer?

And I guess even those aren't the *real* questions. What my mother actually wants to ask is "How do I get you to behave the way I want? What switches do I flip to fix you so that you aren't just one more problem I have to deal with today?"

"Are you feeling sick in your stomach?" She's repeating herself now.

This would go on all day if I let it. But I think I know the answer.

"He doesn't like it when the nurse tussles his hair," I say from the back seat.

"Shut up," my brother tells me.

"What?"

"The nurse," I say. "Every day she comes in and she tussles his hair. She always brings him an extra plate of food. Or candies. Yesterday she tried to pinch his cheek."

"Which nurse?" my mother says. "The one who calls everyone 'dear'?"

"Yes," my brother says. He's still staring out the window, and I can see tears on his cheeks. I don't like to see him so frustrated.

"I don't understand," my mother says. "She seems nice."

"Well, nice or not, it should be up to Simon who gets to tussle his hair."

"Okay," she sighs. "I'll talk to her tomorrow."

Beside me, Simon is silent again.

>_

When we get to the hospital today, the nurse is there. She's just leaving my father's room.

"Good morning," she says, when she sees us. Then, specifically to my brother, she leans down and says, "Good morning, Simon." She reaches out to tussle his hair.

"I don't like to be touched," Simon says very loudly. Her hand stops in mid-air. Even my mother looks shocked.

"Oh." The nurse laughs. "That's okay!"

"I know," Simon tells her. "I know that it's okay. It is up to me who gets to touch my hair. It is not up to you."

"Well, good morning anyway?" The nurse laughs again. She has a look on her face like she might try to tussle his hair again out of embarrassed confusion. Simon's hands are fists at his side and he is staring at her in a way I have never seen him stare at anyone.

"Simon," my dad calls from inside the room. He has no idea what is going on. "Be polite."

"I think he's being very polite," my mother says. She stands closer to her son, and she looks right at the nurse. "It is up to Simon who touches his hair," she says.

>_

Today, while Simon and I went down to the cafeteria to get some jello with cool whip, I left my phone recording. It was just my father and mother, alone in the room. We weren't gone for very long, and so there wasn't a lot for me to transcribe. Except, right before Simon and I came back upstairs, you can hear my parents kiss.

"I love you," my mother says. Very quiet. Almost too quiet to hear. She doesn't sound sad, exactly. Even though she sounds like there are tears in her voice.

<107>

I don't have a word for how she sounds. There's another kiss, and then she says it again, "I love you."

"I don't blame you," my father says.

>_

My mother and I never fight. Usually, I just say what she wants to hear. Even if I don't agree, it is always easier to nod and smile. Always. What's the point in fighting? To prove that I'm right? Right and wrong have no effect on the outcome anyway. She is the mother. I'm the child. So she gets her way. I figured that out years ago, and I have become an expert in getting along. I've become an expert in "Okay."

But not this morning. This morning I couldn't do it.

I couldn't nod and smile and say, "Okay." Because it's not okay. I don't want my father to die.

My father doesn't want to spend the last weeks of his life vomiting in some hospital bathroom. I understand that. There were times, during the last round of treatment, when he was in too much pain to even talk. We just sat there around his bed. The treatment they are offering now is more intense than before. The side effects would be worse. But I don't want my father to die. I don't want my father to die. I don't want my father to die.

I recorded the whole interaction, and now I'm sitting curled up in the closet, listening. I say interaction because it isn't even a conversation. There's no back and forth. I sound like a child throwing a tantrum. I didn't really listen to anything my mother said, I was just waiting for my turn to talk.

"It might give him more time," my mother said, "but it will not save his life, Sunday."

"More time is more time."

"No, it isn't." She's trying to be patient. "Not always."

"This is such bullshit." I keep raising my voice. "How is this hard to understand? The longer he is alive, the more time we get to spend with him. Don't you want more time with him?"

"Of course I do," my mother says. "But not everything is about me."

>_

I'm sitting outside in the dark again, staring at the elephant. The screen door creaks behind me, and my mother joins me on the step. She has a plate of food on her lap. A glass of wine in her hand. She sits close, but not too close. Which is how she treats me when she knows I'm sulking.

"You're missing all the fun," she says, looking out toward the broken-down house.

"I respectfully disagree." I slide to the left, my movement slow and fake, more like sign language than real movement, a clumsy pantomime to let her know she is sitting too close, that I am unhappy. It is an embarrassingly obvious act that I am horrified to watch myself perform.

My mother doesn't even try to hide her amusement.

"Just sitting out here looking at a collapsed house in the dark, eh?" she says. "I could go get you a pen and paper if you want. You could write some poetry about how the house is a metaphor for your poor old heart, crushed under the inescapable weight of passing time? Or you could write down a name for each of the stars in the sky, and by naming them ensure that they might never be forgotten. So they might never be forgotten the way you are forgotten, out here, all alone in the cold?"

I know that I'm not actually angry at my mother. I love my mother, and I love her the most when she's like this, when she has that laugh hidden in her voice. But I don't want to let go of my frustration yet, either. It's comforting to be sitting out here, feeling this way. Like I'm finally feeling the right thing at the right time. She's going to ruin that. She's going to make me laugh.

"I'd like to be alone," I tell her.

"Well, you could always go lie down in that field," she says. "There's lots of room!"

"Maybe I will," I say. And there's an honest-to-god pout in my voice now. Horrifying. Like a little baby, the wailing god of petulance. Again I'm watching myself from outside. A little baby throwing a little tantrum that I am helpless to stop. My mother keeps smiling. Patient and amused. Which is infuriating. Which is meant to be infuriating.

"Does this mean you don't want any potato salad?" she says.

>_

We sit and watch the house that has stumbled in that field. The house isn't doing anything, but the sky behind it is moving, slowly. The light is changing. Everything around the house is changing, while it sits there and does nothing.

Behind us, in my grandmother's kitchen, my uncle Frank does card tricks. His voice carries.

"Is it the jack of spades?" he says. "No? Then what's this under your wine glass?"

A voice answers, too quiet to hear properly. My grandmother.

"It's a business card!" my uncle Frank says. "Interesting. Interesting. Well, maybe we should call the number on it?"

My grandmother says something else, again too quiet.

"No, I'm saying call it." My uncle sounds frustrated now. "Here's my cell phone. Look, I'll call it for you," and then we can hear a phone ringing, which nobody answers. "Aren't you going to answer that?"

"This is too elaborate."

"It isn't elaborate. You just have to answer the phone."

"It's a very good trick, Frank," my grandmother says. "May I have my wine back please?"

Beside me, my mother offers the plate.

"Are you sure you don't want any of this?" she says. She takes a bite of the potato salad, making a satisfied, contented sound. "Mmm." Not too obvious, but more than obvious enough. She would never say

"Eat," would never tell me what to do, is not the type of mother to nag. But this is just as obvious, in its way. Does she think I don't know what she's doing?

When I was little, I saw someone use reverse psychology in a movie, or on some TV show. I was thrilled with the idea, thinking that this new secret knowledge was the edge I needed. Thinking I would finally get the upper hand, thinking for once that I might win.

But when I tried it out against one of my mother's threats to withhold dessert ("I don't even *like* chocolate. Whatever."), I found that, of course, it was just one more way for her to tease me. ("You don't? Oh, that's too bad. I bought these two chocolate bars and everything. I guess I'll just eat both of them.") Neither of us were willing to back down from the deception, so I sat and watched, furious, as my mother ate two whole chocolate bars.

She takes another bite of the potato salad. Then offers it again. It does look good.

>_

"Come inside," my mother says. "Come say hello to your grandmother. Talk to your uncles. Listen to their dumb jokes. One or two more glasses of wine and your grandmother might tell us about her spoon collection."

"Well, you got me," I say, already regretting the bitterness in my tone. "My one weakness. Collectable spoons."

"Oh, I see. You're too cool for spoons now. I understand."

"They're spoons."

"Your grandmother has the most badass spoon collection you've ever seen," my mom says. "She's got a whole row of spoons from old mental hospitals. She has a spoon from the Amityville Horror house."

"What, like from the movie?" I can't imagine my grandmother collecting movie props.

"From the actual house. The real-life house. I have no idea what she paid for it. She says she bought it online. And those are just the spoons she has on display. Once, just once, she showed me a spoon that someone used as a murder weapon. She won't say who, or where she got it. It's not even that old. It looks brand new. She has it wrapped in plastic to protect it."

She pauses.

"Anyway, I've said too much. Come hang out with your dumb, weird family," my mom says. "You can't spend the whole night just mooning around in your own brain."

"I can. I can and I will."

>_

"I'll tell you what," my mother says. "If you promise not to be a wet blanket, and if you spend some time with your brother tonight, I will tell you a secret I've never told anyone else."

A wet blanket. The light and noise from inside the house along one side of my mother's face, insects and evening shadow on the other. Her face is serious, but never too serious. Never serious in the eyes, anyway. Everything is funny to my mother, and it makes it hard sometimes to get close, to know what kind of woman she is underneath. She's always laughing.

But I do love secrets.

"Okay," I say.

"You'll come inside? Make an effort? Pretend to be a real human girl who smiles?" She's deadly pretend serious now. Negotiating. And then suddenly, an intentional crack shows warmth underneath. "I love your smile, Sunday, everyone does. When you smile, it reminds me of when you were a baby, and you would pee anywhere you wanted. It didn't matter where you were, or who was holding you. The world was yours to pee on, and not one person complained. You would smile that wonderful smile, and your victim would start smiling, too, soaked in pee. Nobody could resist your charms."

"Okay, I'll come inside," I say, trying not to laugh. "What's your secret?"

"Let me tell you." She scoots closer to me. "The first thing I ever loved about this house was the pond back there." She thumbs the direction. "Reeds and tall grass everywhere. I loved it. Enormous dragonflies, the whole package. There's a little wharf for fishing and tying the laces on ice skates. It was there when your father first brought me home to meet his mother. It was there when he was a small child. It's always been there."

"And?"

"And two years before you were born, I drowned in that pond. I was out swimming at night, drunk and stupid. My feet got tangled in the long grass. I drowned, and I died."

"Like on TV?" I say, but she doesn't answer. "Like, the paramedics told you that you were legally dead for two minutes? You saw a white light at the end of a tunnel? A bearded face appeared in the stars and called to you?"

"I was dead for a whole day," my mother says. "I woke coughing muck on a metal table at the morgue."

"That's stupid," I tell her, trying to figure out the joke.

Across the road, a light comes on in one of the elephant's windows, dim and yellow. There is no car in the drive.

"Nothing stays dead out here," my mother says.

And then she winks.

>_

I have a recording where neither of them talk at all until the very end. You can hear the sound of their breathing, and I think you can hear my mother crying, though I can't be sure. She sniffles, once. It could just be a sniffle. But then, after all that silence, my father clears his throat and it sounds like he's been crying, too.

"You made me very happy," he says.

I shouldn't be doing this, recording them without their knowledge. But it is too late to stop now. This will all go into the virus. A ghost should be filled with secrets anyway, shouldn't it? And by recording everyone, I get to hear parts of him that are hidden from me. Parts of him that are only for Simon, only for my mother. Only for my uncle Frank.

"You get cancer yet?" my father says. He makes the same joke whenever Frank comes in to visit.

"No, not yet."

"Well, don't worry. You will. Maybe next year is your year."

"Or maybe it isn't genetic?" Frank says. "Maybe it's based on merit?"

They laugh.

But the recordings of my father and mother alone are the ones that feel the most personal. That feel the most important. I've gotten good at hiding my phone.

Monday:

"I wish I could come with you," my mother says.

"I'm not going anywhere," my father says. "I'm dying. When I die, that's it. The end. Cut to black."

"I know," my mother says. "I'm saying that sounds nice."

Thursday:

"I want Sunday to write my obituary," my father says on the recording. "I already asked her."

"I thought Frank was working on something?" My mother's voice. "I thought things were better between you?"

"They are, but I want Sunday to write it."

Friday:

"I won't be back in time to see you tonight, love," she says.

"Well, then I guess this is goodbye forever."

"Goodbye forever," my mother says.

Maybe I should feel jealous, hearing my mother say those secret words. But I'm not.

"Well, then I guess this is goodbye forever." I play it back again and again.

"Goodbye forever," my mother says. "Goodbye forever. Goodbye forever. Goodbye forever." Over and over again until it doesn't mean anything. "Goodbye forever."

>_

In the car, I record Simon and my mother singing a song. One of the waif's endless supply of Muppet songs. It isn't the cleanest recording in the world. You can hear the white noise hum of the car driving. The occasional thump of a pothole. But you can also hear my mother laughing and Simon practically hollering the words, "Mahna Mahna! Do doo do-doo-doo!" over and over again, all along the road to Tatamagouche. These are things worth recording. In the back seat, Simon keeps getting louder and louder. "Do doo do-doo-doo!"

<128>

"Okay," my mother says, finally. "Okay, that's enough. No more 'Mahna Mahna.' I'm going to lose my mind."

"Well, what should we sing?" the waif says.

"Anything else. Literally, anything else. Maybe something quieter?"

There is a brief pause, and then very quietly the waif starts singing again, doing his Bert voice. "Got my hat on my head. Got my scarf around my neck. I'm all dressed up . . . and ready to gooooooo!"

When we arrive at the hospital, that nurse is there. She steps out from behind her station.

"We've been trying to call you," she says.

"We don't get reception in the—" my mother starts, but she stops when she realizes what's happening. "Oh," she says.

"I'm sorry." The nurse reaches out for my mother's arm, but doesn't connect. My mother has taken a step backwards. "I'm sorry. He's gone," the nurse says.

Our father is dead, she says.

And then she keeps right on saying it.

<129>

>_

While the nurse talks, my mother listens calmly, with her arm protectively around Simon's shoulder, her other hand holding mine. I try to squeeze back, but it feels like all the strength has gone out of my muscles. Neither Simon nor I are looking at the nurse. We're watching our mother.

Our mother is staring straight ahead, though. She looks almost angry. Eventually, the nurse stops talking and tells us she has to go find the doctor.

"He wanted to speak with you," she says to my mother.

"Of course," my mother says. "Of course."

We watch the nurse go back behind her island, where she picks up a phone. As soon as she looks away, we're moving. My mother takes us to the women's bathroom, pushes the door open, ushers us inside. There, her hand slips away, and she lets out a barking sound. Simon jumps, and I almost laugh. I'm so scared. Our mother lets out another bark, and then she's crying. Loud and ugly, and it sounds more like choking than barking now. She slides down the wall 'til she is sitting flat on the dirty bathroom floor, and she cries and cries while Simon and I stand there and watch. I keep expecting Simon to start crying, too, but he just stands there as stupidly as me. I don't know what to do. Neither of us do. We stand in the women's bathroom and watch our mother sob on the floor until there is spit and tears all over her face.

She cries like we aren't even here.

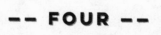

-- FOUR --

In the context of hundreds of pounds of meat and bone and muscle, of course their eyes seem gentle.

The cows are waiting for us to do something alarming. Simon looks even smaller next to these animals. I imagine him astride the largest, sitting proudly in his button-up shirt, the sun shining behind him. Purpose setting those slight shoulders. Why are there no legends of children who ride cows? There should be. We could conquer this whole continent, riding great beasts like these.

"We should name them," the waif says, his hand on a huge flank. I've been scared to touch them, but I do so now. The cow does not rear or buck. It does not snort or gnash. It accepts my touch with the indifference of a giant. Of a machine. I am trying not to think of it as stupid meat and bone and muscle. I am trying not to think of myself as stupid meat and bone and muscle.

"This creature will be called Lydia," I say. "She will be called Lydia the Destroyer. Lydia the Great Flame, and together we will burn the countryside."

"Lydia the Tattooed Lady!" Simon says, and he starts to sing. "Lydia, oh Lydia, say have you met Lydia? Lydia the Tattooed Lady!"

"She's got eyes that folks adore so," I sing, too.

"And a torso even more so!"

We have filled every afternoon this week riding up and down the red asphalt on our bikes. The Malagash Bible Camp. The salt mine memorial. The church, the beaches, the wharves. We've touched every lobster trap. Climbed inside every abandoned rowboat. We spent hours sitting on top of barns, sneakers on hot metal. Fingers tracing rivets.

We should not be this close to animals this large. But who is left to tell us that? There's no sign posted out in this field. Nobody is watching. Our grandmother is on her errands; our mother won't leave her room. We are subject to no authority, my brother and I. We are free. Governed only by what little sense we were born with.

>_

We wander up and down the rows of a vineyard, grape vines that grow taller than us. We walk in separate rows, so that we are just our voices. Simon's voice is high and strong now. It feels stronger every day. We spend all our time together now, just the two of us, talking and making stupid jokes. Filling the hours with our company.

The dirt at the bottom of every row is dark today, still wet from this morning's rain. This vineyard is three fields over from our grandmother's house, and we usually stop here on our way out farther or on our ride back home. Like a pit stop. The grapes are too sour to eat, but we keep trying.

"I know where Dad used to hide his knife collection," I'm saying. "The little table in the living room is a chest. It has all his knives and his hunting rifle. If we ever go home, I'm going to take one."

"Which one?" my brother says.

"I don't know. I haven't decided yet," I say. "The one that feels the most like our father." I try to remember him showing me his knives, try to remember which ones he even had, their shape and size. There was a big military-looking knife. Like a Rambo knife. I remember that. And a switchblade. Which one was the coolest? Which one did our father like best? There were more, I'm sure of it. But I can't picture them. I can only see my father's big goofy grin. "You should take one, too, Simon. He would want you to have one."

"We should ask Mom," my brother says.

I don't say anything to that.

>_

"It's almost lunch," my brother says.

When we emerge from the rows of grapes, I hear an engine in the distance. Two engines. A pair of motorcycles ride along the road, down at the bottom of the field. Headed toward the north point, where they'll loop around. Just passing through. Enjoying the sunshine and the open road. Simon and I stand there and watch until they're out of sight. We're in no hurry.

Our bicycles are just where we left them, twisted in the grass at the bottom of the field. We wheel them up onto the road again, side by side. They aren't really ours. They're too big for us. Simon has to ride standing up to properly reach the pedals. He can't reach the seat. Mine has long tassels streaming from the end of the handlebars. I don't know who they used to belong to. Our father and Frank, maybe? When they were teenagers?

"You can go up around the point now," was the only explanation our grandmother gave when we asked her about the bikes that were leaning against the tree one morning. "Or down as far as the Bible Camp."

The whole ride home from the vineyard, my bike makes a rusted shrieking sound, and the joker card Simon pinned to his back wheel whirrs like a toy engine. They're old, and they're not in the best condition, but they get the job done. We've been all over Malagash on these bikes.

Visiting our dad in the hospital gave our days structure. Now all we have is the sky and red road and sandwiches every day at noon.

We lean the bikes carefully against the driveway tree and let ourselves into the kitchen. Today's lunch is tuna salad sandwiches. With bits of raw onion mixed in. Milk in small glass tumblers with playing card patterns on the glass. Our mother is not here. She's still in her room.

"I'll bring her a sandwich," the waif says, but my grandmother just shakes her head.

"She just needs a bit of space," my grandmother says. "She'll eat when she's ready."

>_

After lunch, we go up to our mom's room and knock.

"Do you want to go for a walk?" I ask through her door. "We saw blue jays down by the water this morning."

"Two of them!" my brother says.

"Not right now," my mother says. Her voice sounds far away. "Maybe later, okay?"

"Or we could dig for clams!" Simon says. "On the beach!"

No answer. We stand there like idiots.

"Lydia, oh Lydia," I start quietly. "Say, have you met Lydia?"

"Lydia the Tattooed Lady!" Simon joins in.

"She has eyes that folks adore so," we sing to the closed door. "And a torso even more so!"

>_

Our mother doesn't come down for dinner, either. The waif and I sit at the table while our grandmother brings us slices of brown bread and glasses of Pepsi. She has a plate of food laid out for herself, just like ours. A pork chop and peas. Mashed potatoes. Baked beans. She doesn't sit, though. Not yet. She sets our glasses in front of us and suddenly realizes that she forgot the chow chow.

I love the food our grandmother makes. Simple, standard dishes. Pork chops. Steak. Ham. Every meal with baked beans and brown bread to scoop them up. On the side, always a dollop of chow. Her pantry closet is stacked with cans of beans and glass jars of pickled green tomato chow. Packets of jello for us to make in the afternoons and eat after our dinner.

"Where did you go today?" she asks us as she works.

"We went out to the end of the wharf," Simon tells her. "And we tried to dig up clams, but we only found tiny baby ones."

"And we saw blue jays this morning," I say.

"I love a blue jay," my grandmother says, lifting the wall phone off the hook and setting the receiver down on the counter. Then she comes around the table and finally sits.

"Why do you take the phone off the hook every day?" Simon asks her. He's smearing too much margarine on his slice of brown bread.

"Because there is nothing in the world more important than having dinner with my grandchildren," my grandmother says.

She shakes pepper and salt onto her food. She takes

a butter knife and puts too much margarine on her brown bread, just like Simon does, and then looks up to smile at us.

"And because it's annoying," she says.

>_

I showed Simon how to access all of the recordings on my computer. Every time he asked me to play him something, I would sit and choose the files for him. I felt weird about that, like I was deciding what he should remember, and when. So when he asked me again, I sat him down at the computer and showed him where the database was. I showed him how to browse the entries or search for specific words. I showed him the tags that meant a recording featured Simon and

Dad. Or Mom and Dad. Frank and Dad. Me and Dad. Just Dad.

I showed him how to list entries by "content."

"Private joke," and "obituary plans," and "warm, warm weather."

I showed Simon how to make a playlist of the files he liked. How to listen to the playlist on a loop. How to fix volume problems, which sometimes happened. How to save his playlist for later. How to give it a title. My brother didn't need me to repeat a single thing. I'm not even sure that he needed me to explain in the first place. But he sat patiently and listened. He was building a playlist before I even moved out of his way.

His hand was so small on the laptop's touchpad.

That was a week ago.

Since then, he hasn't been sleeping at night. We still talk after the lights go out, sometimes about computers, sometimes about our mother or our father. But he doesn't drift off to sleep while we talk anymore.

Instead, I'm the one who falls asleep, drifting off to the sound of his voice. Simon stays up. And when I wake in the morning, the closet door is open. The laptop has moved. The headphones are plugged in, when I know I left them neatly wrapped on the shelf.

>_

Simon didn't go to bed at all last night. He's asleep on the carpet, his body half in and half out of the closet. The headphone cord is twisted around his face, and he is snoring in that quiet, almost delicate way my brother snores. Shy, even in his sleep.

The bunk bed creaks as I climb down.

I know what he's been doing at night, listening to our father's voice. But I'm still curious. I want to know which recordings he's opened. Which jokes in partic-ular, which conversations? I want to know what makes

<151>

him feel better when everyone else is asleep. What makes him feel safe.

He looks so small, curled sleeping around the still-open laptop. The screen has gone to sleep, but it wakes up when I touch a key.

A half-dozen recordings are listed. Simon and Dad. Recordings I made of them in secret. I lift the head-phones up gently. Push them into my ears. I click play.

"Do you believe in heaven?" Simon asks, and you can almost hear my father shaking his head.

"I don't believe in heaven, no," he says.

And there is a long pause as Simon processes that information. "What do you believe?" he says, finally.

"I believe that when we die, we die." Again there is a long pause, and you can hear my brother start to cry. Sniffles at first, and then quiet sobs. My father makes quiet sounds of reassurance. "Hey now," he says. "Hey. We're lucky that we get any time at all. Think of it that way! We're so lucky."

The recording continues a bit after that, but it's just dead air.

>_

"Sunday."

My brother is on the ladder to the top bunk, shaking my shoulder. The sun is shining and I can't remember if it is morning or if I'm waking up from an afternoon nap. He shakes my shoulder again, even though my eyes are open and I'm looking right at him. I am obviously awake.

"What do you want, Simon?"

"I think we should make a playlist for mom," he says. "We could play it on the laptop speakers, and she could hear it through the door. Maybe it would make her feel better the way it makes you and me feel better?"

So we sit down together and we make our mother a playlist. A playlist of jokes and laughter and hellos and goodbyes all mixed up and out of order. I mix everything in.

First is our father's voice, laughing, joking. Making promises. Teasing Simon. And then our mother's voice too. And then it is Simon and me. All of us together, talking about the stupidest things. Working out the details of how many cups of coffee needed to be picked up. Who had forgotten to bring a book for Dad to read. Who was going to get him more crushed ice.

All of us, laughing, saying "Goodbye forever" over and over. As if it didn't mean anything at all. Because it doesn't.

>_

Simon and I sit down on the carpet outside her room, with our backs against the stairway railing. I turn my laptop speakers all the way up. Simon presses Play. The first voice is our father's.

"Well, well, well," he says. "Look who it is. My beautiful wife and adoring children." A pause, and then, "How did you get past security?"

When one recording ends and another begins, there's a little clipping sound as the audio cuts out. As the sound quality changes.

"We need a good nickname for that nurse," our mother says on the recording.

"How about Moose?" my brother says.

"Moose?"

"Yeah, like, I'm not a dear. You're a moose!" Simon explains.

"Simon, I have no idea what you just said." Our father's voice.

Then another:

"It is up to Simon who touches his hair," our mother says, defiant.

And another:

"How come the cat never comes to visit? Is she mad at me?" our father asks, deadly earnest.

"You know why," our mother tells him, just as serious. "You know goddamned well what you did."

A clipping sound again:

"Mahna Mahna."

"Do doo-do doo-doo dah doo-doo das doo-do"

Our mother's laughter.

"No more!" She laughs. "Stop!"

"Mahna Mahna!" Simon sings.

"I will drive this car right off a bridge," our mom says, still laughing. "If you don't stop that song, I swear to god I will kill us all."

"Was that a smile? You can't laugh at my jokes, I'm dying!" our father's voice.

"We know you're dying," our mother says. "God. We know. We know. It's very sad. Why do you think we're pretending your jokes are funny?"

A clip. And then another. And another.

We sit there in the hall, me and Simon, playing voices out of the laptop. There's no answer from the other side of the door.

>_

My grandmother always visited my father when we weren't there, after we had gone home for the day. Like we were taking shifts. She liked to be alone with him. The hospital never seemed to bother her about visiting hours.

I have no idea what they talked about.

I don't have any recordings of my grandmother's voice at all. We don't really talk. That night, sitting on the front steps, my mother told me to go inside and ask her about her spoon collection, but I never did. When I think back, looking for her actual words, all I can recall are questions. Practical daily interactions, making sure that Simon and I are fed, that we are warm enough, comfortable, that we have what we need.

I don't have her voice, but I have recordings where I know my grandmother was there in the room. Family meals, sitting here at the table. Everyone laughing and boisterous. My grandmother's voice isn't on the tape with Uncle Frank and Jonah, but she is the reason my mother says a quiet "sorry" after she swears. She's the sound of cereal being poured while I tease the waif over breakfast. How do you transcribe that?

The only time I ever hear her talk at length is on the phone. I don't understand a thing she's saying, though. It's all in French. She talks to her family every night. Her brothers and sisters, down on the south shore. Our grandmother talks to one or two of them every day. Her French peppered with English phrases and swear words. I've otherwise never once heard my grandmother swear, but on the phone she says "fuck" and "shit" as casually as my father used to.

The only other time I heard my grandmother swear was when I found her at the kitchen table looking through photo albums of my father as a little kid. She looked up when I said her name, but she didn't seem to see me at first. We just stood there. Then after a minute she said "shit" under her breath, wiped the tears off her cheeks, and tried to smile.

>_

"It's quiet without Frank and Jonah around," my grandmother said yesterday. "I'm glad that Frank and your
father had a chance to make peace."

It was the first and only hint that there had been
any tension between Uncle Frank and our father. I'm
so used to people saying things that I don't quite understand. Hinting at history I know nothing about.

But it's the most interesting thing she says on any
of my recordings. It's not an offer of food, or a question about our comfort. It is information. An opinion.

<161>

A glimpse of our grandmother. She said it almost like she was talking to herself, while we sat out on the front steps. Simon beside us, on his knees in the dirt of the rhubarb patch that runs under the big front windows.

The only reason I have this on my phone is because Simon was singing another song. I thought I would record him and play it tonight outside our mother's door.

"Neither one of them could ever let anything go," my grandmother said. "They got that from your grandfather, not from me. Men and their principles. There are more important things in this world than being right."

"What did they fight about?" Simon asked, his voice small on the recording.

But she was done talking about it.

>_

All day yesterday, I kept trying to get my grandmother talking again, to coax something out of her that I could record, could transcribe. But all I got was "Ready for jello?" and "More water?" and "It's six o'clock, Sunday, dear. Why do you keep asking about the time? Do you have an appointment?"

It was Simon who finally got her to actually talk to us.

"How old are you, Nanny?" he said.

"I'm seventy-one years old," she said, and then she smiled. "But I don't feel a day over seventy!"

"You look young!" my brother told her, very seriously.

"I always feel young," she said. "I stopped feeling old a long time ago." She smiled again, but it was an even briefer smile this time. Not a sad smile, but the way it flashed and then faded made it seem that way. "I used to think forty was old. When I was forty, I was living in a small town, raising children. Growing a garden. Volunteering at church bake sales. I was worried that I had turned into my mother, who I never wanted to be. I thought my life was over."

There's a muffled sound here on the recording, which is me making sure that my phone is getting this.

"My sisters were worried about me. I was sad all the time, they said. And that was true. So that spring they took me to Las Vegas, and it was wonderful. I was very excited because I had never travelled. It was the first time I ever went to the United States. And my sisters and I always had fun together, you know. Las Vegas was perfect for us. We drank too much wine. We gambled and we smoked and we wore short dresses and we swore like sailors. We were like teenagers."

She laughed.

"I got us all kicked out of a casino for starting a fight with a girl in a cow costume. We were banned, they told us. Oh it was so much fun. Even in the mornings, when I had the worst headaches of my life, I was so happy."

"You started a fight with a lady in a cow costume?" Simon's eyes are wide.

"Well, I pushed her over." My grandmother laughed. "Like when my brothers joked about 'cow tipping.' I'm sorry. I'm going on and on. I don't know what made me think of all that." Another pause, and then, "Your father would have been forty years old in December."

>_

"You have to close these files down when you're done with them," I say.

Every time I open my computer now, Simon has left a dozen files open on my desktop. I spend half my time just cleaning up after him.

"I'm sorry," he says. "I'll do it now."

"No, it's fine." I close the files, one by one, as Simon comes over to stand beside me. Underneath the sound files, there's a single text file open. It is a section of the virus with transcriptions of Dad talking to Simon, my mother, to me. I know that I did not leave this open. I am careful to never leave the virus open where he could see it. But here it is.

He must have found it.

"What is it?" Simon asks, and I tell him.

I tell him every stupid hope and idea in my head about the computer virus. I tell him that it will be our father's ghost. His memory. His echo. I tell him that a virus need not do harm. That not all self-propagating code is malicious. Our father's virus would never delete files. Would never steal passwords or spy on the intimate moments of strangers. Would not spread like cancer, but like a story. Would slip through fibre optic cables to cross oceans, would pass like radio waves through the walls of houses that nobody even knows are haunted. A ghost story that computers tell one another in the dark.

It all comes spilling out, and I'm so happy to finally be able to tell someone.

Simon listens to every word, and then he ruins everything.

"Won't he be lonely without us?" my brother says.

>_

Simon has so many stories about dumb things he did together with our father. They once spent a whole weekend seeing what would happen when they put different things in the microwave. While Mom and I were away. Our new microwave was unpacked and set up, and the old one was meant to go out with Friday's garbage. They microwaved ice cubes and grapes and DVDs and magnets—anything they could think of— laughing at the sparks, at the startling pop sound, and at one another's shocked faces.

"Promise me you'll never tell your mother," our father said. "She'll be furious that we did this without her."

I thought my virus was a perfect plan. But with one question, Simon changed everything. It was so stupid and obvious.

"Won't he be lonely without us?"

And that was that.

We stayed up all night, working. We went through everything, every recording I had, and we transcribed every word. My voice. My mother's. Simon. Frank. Everything went into the virus. It should be all of us there, living forever on the hard drives of strangers. It should be our whole family echoing down through eternity, singing stupid Muppet songs and laughing at mispronounced words.

My father's story doesn't work if he's the only character. If his ghost is going to live on in computers, if his echo is going to laugh and talk forever, then he shouldn't be alone. My mother's voice should be there with him.

My brother's voice.

My own.

>_

When the sun comes up, we're exhausted. But the virus is ready. Everything is transcribed. Our whole family is in this computer virus. It is the ghost of all of us together.

I have it set up so that Simon only needs to push one button, and it will go out into the world. He doesn't need to understand the scripts. He doesn't need to know how the virus will find its way into other systems. The misleading emails it will send with infected attachments. The infection vectors.

<171>

"All you have to do is hit enter," I tell him.

"And then Dad will be everywhere? He'll live forever?"

"We all will," I say.

Simon thinks about this for a moment.

"Can we both push it?" he says.

And so we reach out our hands together and push the button. The script begins to execute, and the old hard drive makes a quiet sound as it spins up, but that's all. The only output that shows on the screen is the simple confirmation, "OK."

Simon watches, clearly hoping for more, but the screen stays the same.

"Is that it?" he says.